To Mom and Dad

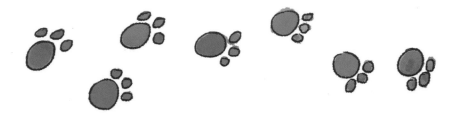

A FEIWEL AND FRIENDS BOOK

An Imprint of Macmillan Publishing Group, LLC

How to Find a Fox. Copyright © 2016 by Nilah Magruder. All rights reserved.

Printed in China by Toppan Leefung Printing Ltd., Dongguan City, Guangdong Province.

For information, address Feiwel and Friends, 120 Broadway, New York, NY 10271.

Our books may be purchased in bulk for promotional, educational, or business use.
Please contact your local bookseller or the Macmillan Corporate and Premium Sales Department
at (800) 221-7945 ext. 5442 or by e-mail at MacmillanSpecialMarkets@macmillan.com.

Library of Congress Cataloging-in-Publication Data
Names: Magruder, Nilah, author.
Title: How to find a fox / Nilah Magruder.
Description: First Edition. | New York : Feiwel and Friends, 2016.
Identifiers: LCCN 2015042041 | ISBN 9781250086563 (hardback)
Subjects: | CYAC: Foxes—Fiction. | BISAC: JUVENILE FICTION / Animals / Foxes. | JUVENILE FICTION /
Social Issues / Self-Esteem & Self-Reliance. | JUVENILE FICTION / Action & Adventure / General.
Classification: LCC PZ7.1.M346 Ho 2016 | DDC [E]—dc23
LC record available at http://lccn.loc.gov/2015042041

Book design by April Ward

The illustrations for this book were created digitally in Adobe Photoshop.

Feiwel and Friends logo designed by Filomena Tuosto

First Edition: 2016

5 7 9 10 8 6 4

mackids.com

HOW TO FiND A FOX

Nilah Magruder

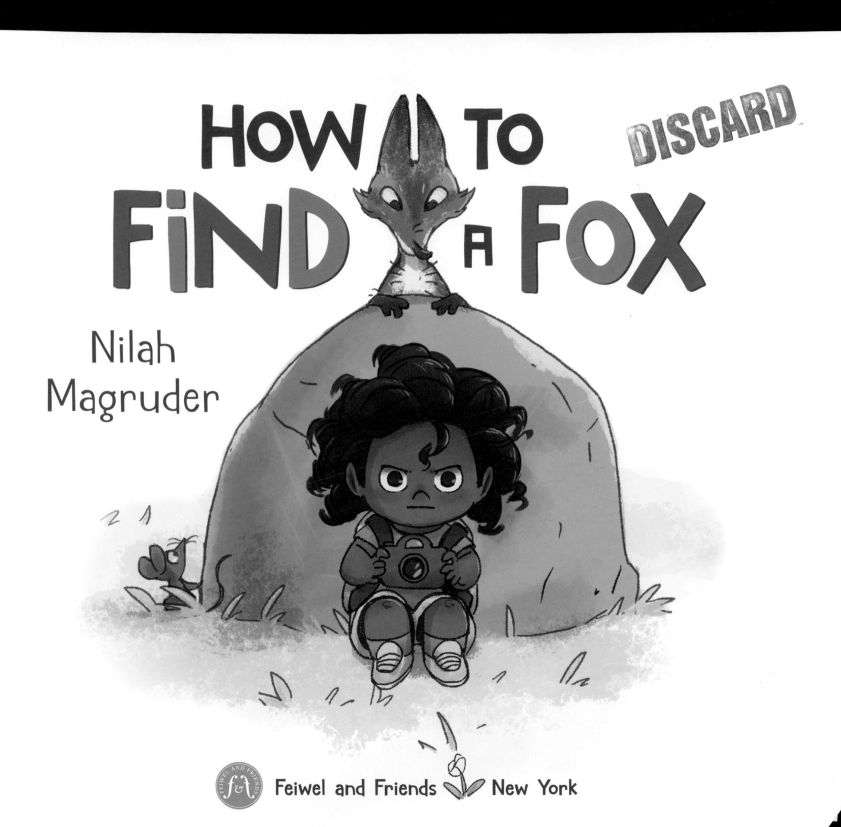

Feiwel and Friends 🌷 New York

How to find a fox:

Find a fox hole.

Any fox hole
will do.

The best foxes are at home
when you visit.

Take out your fox bait.

Place it somewhere easy to spot.

Hide. Then wait very quietly.

Wait a little longer.

Maybe you should try
a different approach.

Tread slowly over the ground.
Foxes have keen hearing.

You don't want to
startle them.

Be sure to look for
fox tracks.

They're like dog tracks,
but sneakier.

Take a picture of a family of raccoons.

They have bushy tails kind of like foxes.

Put out more bait.

Wait longer this time.

Oh no! You waited too long.

Lying around won't bring foxes to you. Keep looking.

Stalk through the grass.
Make fox calls.

Search by the stream. Make more fox calls.

Roll down a hill.
It won't help you find
a fox, but it's fun.

Maybe
you
need
a
change
of
perspective.

Climb
a
tree.

Slowly . . .

Carefully . . .

There he is!

Climb down from the tree.

He's getting away!

Run, run!

You've got to be quick.

Don't lose him!

You lost him.

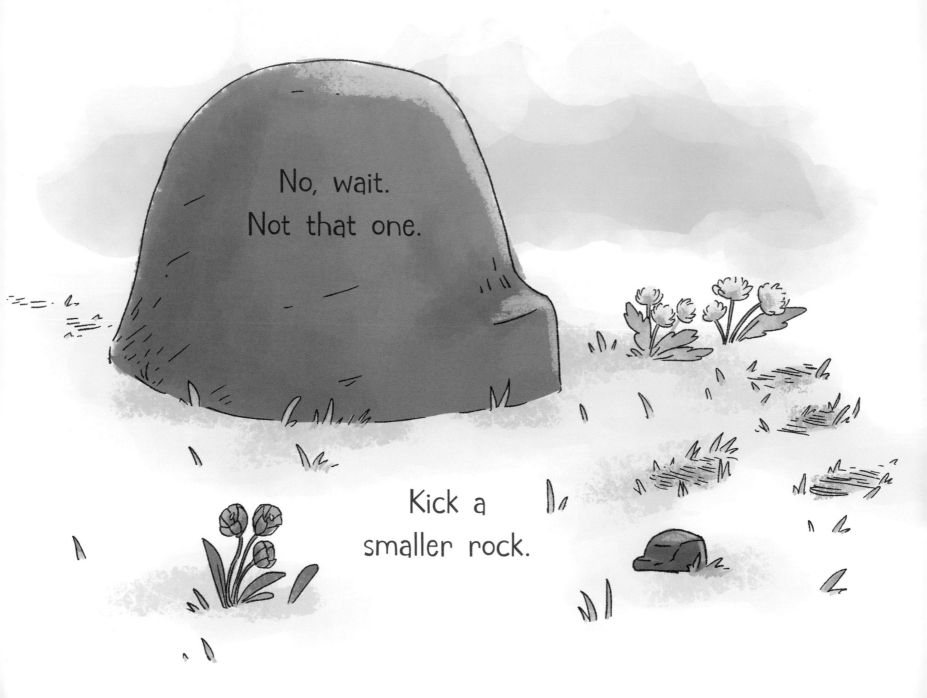

Lie down on your back because it's hopeless.

Perhaps this was the wrong day to find foxes.

Maybe you should just give up.

You want to go home,

but you're too tired.

What do you do now?

You've got a feeling that it's staring you right in the face.....

Some days, a fox doesn't want to be found.

Some days, he wants to find YOU!

Congratulations! You are a
master at finding foxes!